Old Man's Gold
❧ *and Other Stories*

Old Man's Gold
⚹ *and Other Stories*

by Ovid Pierce

The University of North Carolina Press
Chapel Hill

Library of Congress Cataloging in Publication Data

Pierce, Ovid Williams.

  Old man's gold, and other stories.

  CONTENTS: Gub'ner Green.–Midnight prayer.–One of
the darkies. [etc.]
  I. Title.
PZ4.P6170l   [PS3566.I39]   813'.5'4   75-19101
ISBN 0-8078-1257-9

For my friend
JOHN DALE EBBS
with my lasting thanks
and with affection
to my old editors and friends
at Southern Methodist University
who encouraged these early starts:
CLAUDE ALBRITTON
GEORGE BOND
ALLEN MAXWELL
MARGARET HARTLEY
LON TINKLE
ELIZABETH KNIGHT
and ELISE KOONSMAN

Contents

Preface

꧁꧁꧁ I read through these stories this morning. Frankly, I went back to them a little reluctantly. For after half a lifetime I wasn't sure what I'd find. But what I did find appealed to me in a way I hadn't expected. I felt I was looking across a lifetime of change, at the limitations of my own youthful insights, at the limitations of an unthreatened climate, wherein the South, as a subject for fiction, beckoned still in intriguing myth.

I am so completely aware of what these stories are not that I am compelled to ask whether they still hold interest for others. They are frail stories for these quickened times. I see their appeal in such a personal light that I ask for the privilege of putting them in personal perspective. It would not be right to publish them with any assertion of an importance which they do not have.

First of all, written as they were thirty and thirty-five years ago, they show me how far back some of my own paths began. But they show also how far the world itself has come. They testify to the existence of a long ago place and time. It seems likely now that they couldn't have been written earlier than they actually were, nor could they have been written at any later time. Perhaps their value lies just in this. They help to

[x]   Preface

define the innocence of an age. And all ages sit in judgment
upon all others, as much in what they do not reveal as in what
they do.

Ovid Pierce

Old Man's Gold
৯ *and Other Stories*

☖ Gub'ner Green

"What was dat?"

Zeke Jackson almost sprang from his cot, throwing off his cover, baring his body to the night air. His eyes sought a spot at the foot of his bed. Something had been standing there a moment ago! Now it had gone. Zeke moistened his dry lips. Could it have escaped through a window? The long row of gray openings upon the dark wall took definite shape before his eyes. The bars across them were black, secure, against the early morning sky. Then to the door! But there the same old slit of light shone just as always beneath the upper hinge.

He turned quickly and looked up and down over the bodies of the sleeping men. Not one of them stirred. Had they not been waked? Zeke heard no break in the dull heavy rhythm of their snoring. A chill of fear crept over him. If he waked the man lying nearest him, he could hear a human voice. The sound of a human voice would assure him that—but just as he was about to grasp the bed, he held his hand. Those strange words, spoken a moment before, were coming back to him.

"Lawd," Zeke murmured, "was dat *really* You dat was talkin'

Southwest Review 22 (Summer 1937): 366-75.

to me? Dat said I was gonna git free from dis jail? Was dat *really* You?"

Zeke shook his head, thinking he could clear his thoughts. He placed his feet on the floor. The cement was cold to his touch. No, he wasn't asleep. There was no doubt about that. Remembering the water bucket kept at the door, he got up noiselessly, without looking for his shoes, and passed at the feet of the sleeping prisoners. There was Joe asleep, stretched to his full length, and Tom Spinney, with his head half-buried under his pillow, and Oscar lying flat on his back, his mouth wide open and his cover heaped upon the floor—all of them dead to the world.

But suppose somebody in this room wasn't asleep, had been watching him from some dark corner? Zeke's first impulse was to turn about, to get back as quickly as he could to the cover of his bed. But that was foolish—he had only a step or two to go. The water bucket was almost within his reach. As he took the dipper from its nail upon the wall he was seized again by a sudden horror of attracting attention to himself, a fear of striking the dipper against the tin bucket. His hand trembled. But what was wrong with his getting a drink of water during the night? That was what it was put there for. He sank the dipper ever so carefully into the water and drank. In his ears the gulps sounded like pebbles dropping into a lake ten feet below. Through the hall-door transom he heard the scraping of a chair over the cement floor and the low voice of one of the guards speaking to another. Zeke held the water in his mouth. At that instant he wouldn't dare swallow it.

As soon as he could he got into bed and drew the blanket over his face. With warmth and darkness a feeling of security and relief came over him. He sighed heavily. For a while he'd be free to think about this strange thing that had happened.

Although the sun had almost risen Zeke fell into a sound

sleep, for when the first morning bell rang he leapt from his bed, startled. For a moment he was unable to recall where he was. Discovering that he was the only man in the room upon his feet, he sank back upon his cot and looked about to see if he'd been watched. For the most part the men were still stretching and yawning. Some few of them at the other end of the room were sitting up, looking down at their feet. Near him, Joe Perkins, lying about five feet away, was sufficiently awake to have noticed him.

"What ails you, Zeke?" Joe muttered.

Zeke answered readily, "I swear, I blieve sumpin's bitin in dis bed."

"Hunh, it ain't the bites dat bothers me. It's dese here mattresses. When you turn over it don't give no more than a sidewalk do. Bet I ain't slept a good hour all night long."

"Hunh?"

"I say I bet I ain't slept more'n a hour all night," Joe repeated.

"How come?" Zeke turned to him directly.

"Ain't no perticler reason, I reckon. I just had it in my mind dat I was a-hearin sumpin. Mought not been no more 'n a bad dream."

"I didn't have no dreams," Zeke spoke out quickly. "I ain't never slept better in all my life. Last night I was so tired out dat when I hit dis bed I bet I ain't turned over till that bell rung. Naw-suh, I was dead to dis worl. I ain't heard nothin and I ain't seen nothin."

"Well, I didn't say I heard a racket goin on all night. I just said I didn't exactly know what it was myself. Sumpin just kinder kept me awake. Fer all I know it mought er been dem fried taters I et."

This admission brought only a moment's peace to Zeke's mind. But he went on with his dressing, fearing he'd give himself away by asking too many questions. "If there was anything goin on, danged if I know what twuz," he said finally.

"Who said anything was goin on?" Joe demanded. "I ain't said nothin of the sort."

"Well, I ain't trying to argue wid you," Zeke said. One thing was sure, from now on he was going to have to keep his eye on Joe Perkins.

At that moment came the signal for the men to take their places in line. One of the guards stationed himself inside the room, within a foot of the water-stool. Just as he was ready to begin the checking he looked down and saw he was standing in a puddle of water. For a second or two he didn't look up, then he turned towards the men. "I've put up with this thing just about as long as I'm going to. Who was the last man to use this dipper?" He picked it up and held it for them to see. No one answered. "Who threw this water on the floor, I say?" Still there was no answer. "So I don't reckon a damn one of you has had a drink of water in a week?"

The men in line began to look from one to another. Some of them shook their heads.

"I ain't touched the dipper."

"Ain't no use to look at me. I ain't throwed no water on the floor."

"Nawsuh, I ain't drunk out that dipper since I been here."

By this time Zeke was in line, looking straight ahead, absorbed by something he saw upon the wall. Was he the only one in the whole crowd who had not spoken?

"Well, come on! Get moving!" The guard took a pencil from his pocket and began checking the numbers as they passed.

"Thirteen."

"Hyah."

"Fourteen."

There was no answer. The guard looked up from his paper into the face of the next prisoner. "Well, what's eatin you?"

"That ain't my number, boss. I'se fifteen."

The man behind Zeke nudged him in the back. "You'se out of place. Git up there quick!"

Number Fifteen turned round and saw Zeke behind him. "How come you got us balled up like this, Zeke?"

"I'se fourteen, boss," Zeke exclaimed.

"Well, why in the hell don't you keep in your place? Get where you belong and get the devil out of here."

"Yassuh."

Zeke's heart was thumping against his ribs. In his excitement he began mumbling to himself.

"Who you talkin to, Zeke?" asked the man in front of him.

"Hunh?"

"I say who you talkin to? I don't blieve you'se wake good yit."

"Yes I is, too. Bet I ain't never slept better in all my life."

Zeke was sent down to the cornfield. When noon came he hardly knew how the morning had passed, it had gone so quickly. But later on when the muscles of his back and arms began to ache he realized he must have spent four good hours chopping like the devil. Several times during the afternoon he caught himself resting, leaning upon his hoe, staring into the distance. Once, halfway down one of the corn rows, he stopped to look up at the sun. Instead of blueness there was nothing overhead but a mass of tangled corn leaves, narrow flecks of blue showing through them. The stalks were so high and so heavy with foliage that Zeke was cut off from the world. Who would ever have thought a man could hide in an open field! For a moment or two he stood still. He heard the voices of other men round him. Several rows away a prisoner was chopping. Zeke could hear the sharp crunching of the blade as it dug into the crusty soil, an occasional clacking scrape as it hit upon a rock. From a distance he heard the low unintelligible song of another prisoner, and from a greater distance came the yapping of a dog. Stealthily he thrust his head through a mass of the long green blades and peered to the right and left. Not a soul could see him. "Lawd," Zeke whispered, "was dat *really* You?"

After supper Zeke stood in the doorway by himself and watched the other men walking about the enclosure. Then he went inside and lay down upon his cot. It was all he could do to keep from falling asleep. As he lay there he heard the indistinct, idle talk of the men outside the window and every now and then, after a single voice had spoken at length, he heard a burst of free, happy laughter. And, then, suddenly, he heard his own name spoken.

He raised up. Tom Spinney was standing near the door. He was talking to a group of men, earnest faces turned towards his.

"You call me, Tom?"

"Hit don't make no diffunce," Tom answered, looking back over his shoulder at Zeke. "Hit don't concern you none nohow."

Zeke got up.

Tom Spinney was saying to the men: "I know hit's de truth. I heard him say so myself. I swear fore God and hope to die fore sunrise if he didn't say dey was gonna be pardoned tomorrow. Go in dare and ast Mister Brooks hisself if you don't blieve me."

"Well, how come you can't tell us who dey is then?" asked Henry Buckner.

Several repeated the question. One said: "Sure, if you know so much, how come you don't know who they is?"

"I done tole you three times," Tom said. "I don't care whether you blieve me or not. Hit don't make no diffunce to me. All I know is dat he said de gub'ner has already sent de papers down fer two prisners to git out tomorrow."

With that he turned away from them and met Zeke, face to face.

Zeke had been standing there behind him, listening.

"Git out er my way, Zeke," Tom said. "What ails you?"

Zeke started to answer but was afraid his voice would betray him. He stood there and looked out through the open doorway. His heart was full. He knew he'd been sinful in doubting the words of the Lord. But how was he to know he could believe a dream? The Lord had really, really meant it.

A while later, the room dark and the eyes of his fellow prisoners closed, his thoughts turned to the days ahead of him. The first thing he'd have to do when he got out would be to patch up his barn and build a new chimney for the kitchen. Zilphy wouldn't come back to him until he'd done that. He'd have to fix it up nice before she'd come. But she would come, there wasn't any doubt about that. Her Pa wouldn't want her to, but if he fixed the house up nice, she'd come back. She'd certainly come back. If he could just borrow a little money, he could buy a mule. That was all he needed to start. Just one mule. He'd have a crop in no time. And they could plant a garden. Why, someday he might even buy her a Ford car. Zilphy would come. She'd have to!

The first light of morning woke him. He sat up in bed. The men around him were sleeping. Zeke looked at them as they slept. This was his last morning. Now that he was leaving them he could forget all the mean things they'd done. Even those who had been spiteful he forgave. They were all right. They were all pretty good fellows.

Then Zeke prepared himself for the day. It was almost sunrise; it would be only a few hours now. He might be told about it at breakfast time. Already he could see the warden, standing at the head of the table, an important look upon his face. He could hear him clearing his throat and speaking out: "Zeke Jackson, prisoner number fourteen, is wanted on business at the office." Then the warden would turn and go out of the room. Yessir, that's how it would be! It would mean he was a free man! And as soon as he got his papers, he'd have to come back here to get his clothes. There'd be some money coming to him, too. It wouldn't be much. But it would be something! Maybe it would be enough to make a payment on a mule.

An hour later the prisoners marched in to breakfast. They stood behind long benches before an uncovered table. Zeke fastened his eyes upon the knob of the door through which the warden would enter. In a second he would enter. In a second he would come. But first the knob would turn. Zeke kept his eyes upon it. Was it footsteps he heard? Seconds passed. Could it be from the other side of the room that he entered? He looked from one door to another. The men round him were sitting down. Lord, where was the warden? Everybody was seated. A full minute had gone. Zeke took his place at the table and began to eat. He did not know what he was eating. There had been a mistake. Was it possible that they didn't tell the prisoners in the morning that they would be freed that day? Did they wait till twelve o'clock, when the men came in from the fields, to tell them? Yes, that was it! Sure, that was it! They always waited till twelve o'clock. Didn't Henry Cassidy have to wait till twelve o'clock before he knew he was free?

The guards were waiting in the yard for the prisoners. They carried rifles slung under their arms. They were spitting tobacco juice into the dust. Sometimes the spit would roll over and over like a little ball wrapping itself up in dust. Zeke spat down at his own feet. One red-faced guard came down the line, looking over the men. He stopped in front of Zeke, then turned to speak to another guard: "How many men d'you need in the cornfield down on the river?"

"We need more'n we had the other day. Gimme a dozen."

"Here, you," the guard on horseback shouted, pointing to Zeke. "You and the next four in line go along with the corn gang. Give him your number over there by the gate. And, Johnson, you take the rest of 'em and git started in the cotton where you left off last week."

The prisoners formed into several groups of twelve, with two guards over each group. The gates had been opened. The little companies set out in different directions over the broad fields. Zeke kept his eyes to the ground. He saw nothing but the slow fall of his own feet into the inch-thick dust. It was getting hot. He felt the sun upon his back; he was completely dazed by it. This day was beginning like the day before and the day before that. Here were the same men round him. The same fields. And over him the same guards. It wasn't the way for this day to begin. Was it possible that his dream had not been real?

A thirty-acre field of corn lay in the low grounds near the river. It was bordered on the north by a thicket of pines and underbrush, beyond which a slow muddy river flowed by to the sound. Looking down upon this field from the high ground on which the prisoners were standing, Zeke saw a glittering sea of green leaves. Thousands of slender blades were inviting, rising, falling. Suddenly a light wind blew across them in a narrow path. It left a trail of sunlight upon the upturned leaves.

"Git yo hoes and start down this row where we left off!" shouted the guard. "An work fast so we can git away from here by twelve o'clock."

The men picked up their hoes and walked singly across the fields. The guards took their positions: one on horseback, looking down the rows, the other at the far end of the field. Without looking, Zeke knew he was midway between the two. The prisoner working nearest him was Isaac Jones, a man of about Zeke's age. Zeke knew things had closed around him. He raised his hoe and let it fall in the crusty soil. Now it was as always. All the hope and happiness of his heart had gone, leaving in their place a sickening dread. The promise that twelve o'clock held roused in him nothing more than a thin unexciting wonder.

Finally, turning to Isaac, he said:"Isaac, didn't Tom Spinney say last night that two men was gonna be set free today? Didn't he say that de gub'ner was gonna pardon em?''

'Sho, de gub'ner pardoned em,'' Isaac answered. ''Didn't you see em when dey left?''

''Hunh?''

''Didn't you see em when dey left?'' Isaac repeated.

''They gone?''

''Sure, they gone. They drove off in a Ford car this morning.''

''And so it wasn't me that the gub'ner was gonna pardon?''

''Twan't you?'' Isaac said. ''I swear and be damn! It don't look like you, do it? Zeke you ain't got the sense God give a turkey-buzzard. The sun has sure gone to yo head.''

''And so de gub'ner ain't gonna give me no pardon?''

Isaac stopped hoeing. He took a step or two closer to Zeke and saw the sweat rolling from his face.

''What's ailin you, Zeke? Git out an ask the man to let you lay down.''

''Hish, Isaac,'' Zeke murmured. ''I had a dream from the Lord. The Lord said He was gonna set me free. He said the gub'ner was gonna open the gates an I was gonna walk out.''

''Hish, nigger.''

''He said de gub'ner was gonna set me free.''

''Zeke, has you had a sho-nuff vision?''

Zeke stooped over within close range of Isaac's ear. ''There is another gub'ner, Isaac. There is Gub'ner Green. You see these here cornstalks? Ain't they higher than a man's head? Won't they hide a nigger when he's runnin? How does I know the Lord didn't aim for me to run? Ain't this here cornfield just as good as a gub'ner?''

"Zeke, is you gone crazy?"

"Ain't this the pardon the Lord was talking bout?" Zeke murmured. He gathered the long slender blades over his head and pulled them down to hide his face. "Don't the Lord know what He's doin?"

"Zeke, you gonna git shot!" Isaac's words were hoarse. He drew back several steps.

Zeke turned from Isaac and looked in the direction of the mounted guard, who was sitting there flicking flies from his horse's neck. The other guards were lost to his sight behind the corn rows. Zeke saw a path opening before him across the field. His vision over the waving stalks was beckoning.

"Zeke, you're a fool!"

Were the guard's eyes upon his back?

He put out one hand to push aside the first stalk across his path. His feet would not move. "Oh, God," he said, "I saw You. But I can't see You no more."

The sun and the fields were turning black. The path which had opened before him was now a tangle of green blades. He dropped his head into his hands.

When Isaac reached him he had fallen to his knees.

"It ain't no use, Isaac," he was whispering. "I'll stay here for a hundred years."

"Zeke, Zeke, git up! The guard's comin!"

"I ain't gonna run," he said.

"What's the matter with that man?" asked the guard.

"I ain't gonna run, boss. I swear I ain't! I'll stay here, honest to God, I'll stay here for a hundred years."

"I say, what's the matter with that man?"

"Somethin's got him, boss," Isaac said.

"He's crazy, ain't he?"

"Honest to God, boss, I'll stay here for a hundred years!"

"Who said anything about stayin here a hundred years?"

"I'll stay, boss, I swear, I'll stay."

The guard looked down at Zeke for a moment, then he called to the other guard on the far side of the field. "Hey, Pete, come over here a minute! A man's had a sunstroke."

☙ Midnight Prayer

It had been a long hot walk. When Hessie reached the shade of the lime tree, she stopped to cool her feet in the light sandy soil. There were no other shadows upon this sun-colored yard. As she stood there she raised her apron and wiped the sweat from her face; then she looked up at the big white house at the edge of the grove and, after a while, walked into the sun again.

The moment she came within calling distance she turned her face to the second-floor windows. "Oh-h-h, Muster Stan!"

Most Negroes would have sat on the back steps all afternoon, waiting, before they would have dared wake Mr. Stan from his nap.

"Hish hollerin dat way at dem windows!" came a voice. "You know ez good ez I do dat Muster Stan is 'sleep.'"

Hessie was prepared for this. She turned her head slowly towards the kitchen window on the first floor. The window framed the smooth, chocolate-colored face of Corsetta.

"Corsetta," Hessie said, "when I wants you I'll holler twards de kitchen. But when I wants Muster Stan I'm gwine holler twards de house. Ain't nobody lookin fer you *yit*!"

Southwest Review 23 (January 1938): 189-99.

"What you want wid Muster Stan, anyway?"

Hessie smiled mysteriously and went on calling: "Oh-h-h, Muster Stan!"

"Hish, I done tole you," Corsetta commanded. Her voice was as loud as Hessie's. "You ain't got no more manners dan a hawg—come a-hollerin here dis time a day. Muster Stan ain't gonna wake up from his sleep jist to come down here and hear you jawin."

"Lemme tell you somethin, Corsetta," Hessie said.

"What?"

"Dare ain't no argument bout it. You is jist whar you wanter be. You is set up in dat kitchen ez cook. You is what dey call de white folkses nigger—"

"What you aimin at, Hessie? Tain't nothin but yo big mouf."

"You gwine see whose big mouf it is." Then she turned away as if she'd said all she intended.

Corsetta did not move from the window. "I boun you ain't up to no good," she said, after a moment.

The woman on the steps ignored the remark. "Why don't he come on down here?" she muttered to herself. Flies had begun to swarm about her head. She fanned at them halfheartedly and took her seat on the steps. "I kin sit till he do come," she said. For the minute her attention was drawn to a number of Plymouth Rock hens pecking at watermelon seeds round the steps. One of them came close to her toe. "Git away from here!" She kicked towards them and the chickens fluttered and cackled. "When I was cookin in dis house I didn't allow no chickens round de back door."

"When you was cookin in dis house Muster Stan couldn't keep no chickens. Das de only reason dare won't none at de back door. Wouldn't a-been no hawgs neither iffen you could a-toted em off."

"Das a lie and you know it." As she spoke the door opened behind her. She turned quickly.

A short, stout man, his face flushed, his gray hair matted to his forehead, was standing there blinking down at her. "What d'you want with me, Hessie?"

Hessie stood up, glanced at Corsetta, then back at Mr. Stan. "I ain't aimin to cause no trouble," she said. "It ain't none of my business nohow. I knows ez how you don't allow no foolishness, but I come by to pass on to you what I done heard."

"Well, get on with it."

Corsetta leaned farther out of the window.

"I was a-thinkin mebbe you mought want a cook in de mawnin."

Corsetta jerked her head back and bumped it on the window. "Listen here, Hessie," she shouted, "don't you start nothin round here! I'll break yo neck!"

"Keep quiet, Corsetta!" Mr. Stan came out on the porch. "Hessie, what d'you come here for?"

Hessie continued: "Cose it ain't none of my business. I don't know nothin bout such stuff. But I can't keep from hearin, kin I?"

"Hearin what?"

"Bout Corsetta," she said firmly.

"Hessie, I swear to Gawd, I'll, I'll—"

"Hush, Corsetta!"

"Lawd Gawd, Muster Stan, don't let em do dat to me. Pray Gawd, don't let em do it."

Mr. Stan looked from one woman to the other. "What the devil is all this about?"

"All I knows is what Brer Hepps tole me," she answered. "He done tole me dis mawnin dat Sister Corsetta is conjured. Das all I knows."

"Conjured?"

"Listen here, Hessie, I'll have you locked up if you start that foolishness around here. You cause me more trouble than anybody on the plantation. Now you listen here to me—"

"Muster Stan, don't let em do dat to me! Please Gawd, don't let em work no spell on me! I ain't done nothin to them. All dey wants is my job in de kitchen. If Hessie don't git away from here I'm gwine cut her thoat!"

"Don't be a fool, Corsetta. Nobody can conjure you."

"I ain't aimin to start no trouble, Muster Stan," Hessie said. "I ain't done nothin in de worl cep tell you what Brer Hepps done tole me."

"Make her git away from here, Muster Stan! Make her git away!"

"Hessie, I got a good mind to have you put in the lock-up. Now you go on and get out of my yard with all that damn foolishness! And don't you come back here any more, d'you hear me?" Mr. Stan took two steps down and shook his finger in her face. "I'm not gonna put up with such stuff around here. Now get out! Go on away from here right this minute! Right this minute! D'you hear me?"

Hessie drew back. "It ain't me, Muster Stan. It ain't me, I swear to Gawd! You ast Brer Hepps!"

"I don't give a damn about Brer Hepps! He's as big a fool as you are. You and Brer Hepps put together haven't got sense enough to bell a buzzard!"

"Dey kin conjure, Muster Stan!" Corsetta cried. "I know dey kin, caze I seen em conjure my Ma." She drew back from the window, an ancient fear awakened in her breast.

Mr. Stan waited on the steps until Hessie, with her pinched, waspish face, had backed away, muttering to herself under the hot sun.

Then he went into the kitchen. "Now listen here, Corsetta, don't let's have any foolishness about this thing. You go on and tend to your business and don't pay any attention to her. She can't do anything to you."

But Corsetta knew better than Mr. Stan. She had seen it too

many times not to believe in the magic of this dark world in which she and her people lived.

Late in the afternoon, as soon as she had finished her work, she left for home. Her two-room cabin, where she lived with her husband and two children, lay across an open field about half a mile from Mr. Stan's. She reached there just before nightfall, fully resolved on the course she should take. Tobe and her two little boys had not yet come in from the fields. She warmed over some food for them and left it with a lighted lamp on the kitchen table. Then she went out into the night, set upon a plan which she knew had saved her mammy and her mammy's mammy long before her.

The summer moon was now high, and the shadows of the trees were threatening and alive. Corsetta took the middle of the road, as far from the shadows as she could get. Every time a cloud sailed over the moon she stopped in her tracks until it passed. When she'd walked for more than two miles she turned aside at a little path that led through a thicket into the woods. Darkness here was thick. She quickened her steps, and hardly more than halfway through she began to run. Finally she saw ahead of her, through the trunks of the trees, the soft yellow shine of a backwoods light. It came from the window of a one-room cabin.

The cabin stood in a small cleared space which, now, almost like a cup, was filled with moonlight.

For a moment Corsetta paused, and her resolve was renewed. Then she rapped lightly at the door, which was standing an inch or two ajar but was secured on the inside by a heavy chain.

"Who is dat?" A hoarse, startled voice came from the far side of the room.

"It's me, Mam Maggie," Corsetta answered. "Dis here is Corsetta."

"Das who?"

"Corsetta."

She heard the slow, deliberate tread of Mam Maggie's bare feet across the floor. The chain in the door scraped against the iron hook, and Mam Maggie thrust her head outside.

"What you come here for dis time o' night?" The old woman was stooped, her face the color of a crusted locust. She wore a dingy cloth round her hair. Her apron was tied high above her waist and fell, barrellike, almost to the floor. "What you come here for dis time o' night?" she repeated.

"Please lemme in. I'se in trouble."

Mam Maggie opened the door wider and admitted her.

This single room and its age-old furnishings were the earthly possessions of Mam Maggie. A big four-poster bed covered the better part of half the floor space. Against the opposite wall was a row of nondescript chests and boxes. In the center wall, across from the door, was a deep fireplace. A slow hickory fire was burning. A kettle hung from a suspended rod over the blaze. The wide, sunken hearth held a pot and two pans.

"What's ailin you, chile?"

Corsetta sank on a chair by the hearth. "I'se tired," she answered.

"Naw, naw, I mean what you come to me for?"

Corsetta began to cry.

Mam Maggie had seen this too many times to allow it to alarm her. She took the other chair near the hearth, picked up a cup and began to drink her coffee. She held her cup in both hands and closed her eyes as she drank. She knew she would hear, in time, why Corsetta had come.

After a while Mam Maggie pulled a small box from under the head of her bed. She took from it a bit of root, the color of cinnamon, and dropped it in the cup from which she had drunk. Then she filled the cup with boiling water from the kettle.

"Here, chile."

Corsetta took the cup.

"When it cool off, drink it."

Corsetta blew into the cup and began to sip.

"Now tell me yo ailment."

She rubbed the back of her hand over both her eyes and looked across at the old woman. "I'se conjured," she said.

None but the conjured came to her. This was not what Mam Maggie wanted to know. "Who done it?"

Corsetta began to cry again. "I'se just conjured. Das all I knows." She placed the cup on the hearth. "I knowed twuz comin, caze dey all wants my job. Dey all been tryin to git it. Dey ain't give me no peace in three years. I done prayed to de good Gawd, I swear I is. But He ain't hear me. All my life I been lookin for it. An all my life I ast de good Gawd to hep me. Please, Mam Maggie, for sweet Jedus' sake, hep me."

"Where you ail?" Each of Mam Maggie's questions was a practical one to bring Corsetta back to the practical business of getting cured.

"I ain't ailin yit," she sobbed.

"Well, how does you know den dat you is conjured?"

"Hessie tole me. She come by to ast Muster Stan iffen he want annuder cook. She say dat by mawnin Corsetta ain't gonna be dare. Das all I knows, cepin I feels it comin. I knows it."

"Is you got a swellin?"

Corsetta grasped at her stomach and sides. "Naw'm, I can't feel no swellin."

"Is you got a knockin in de haid?"

Corsetta jerked her head to the side as though to listen for the pain. "I can't feel no knockin," she said.

"Take off yo left-side shoe," Mam Maggie commanded.

"I didn't wear none," she said, and thrust out her left foot.

"Hist hit up here on my lap and lemme see it."

Corsetta drew her chair closer to Mam Maggie and raised her foot into her lap. Then Mam Maggie leaned over and held each of the toes, one at a time, with her thumb and forefinger. Finally she looked up into Corsetta's eyes. "You ain't conjured, chile. Yo left foot has got de marks which ward off de spell. Yo mammy had de same marks." Corsetta's face brightened into a smile. "But wait a minute. Dat ain't all."

"What you mean by dat?"

Mam Maggie pushed Corsetta's foot away and gazed into the fire.

"Tell me what you mean by dat?"

Mam Maggie turned her head slowly. "Has you ever had any chullen?" she asked.

"Yassum, I got two."

"Dat's de thing."

"What you mean, dat's de thing?" Again her glistening eyes showed alarm. She leaned over to catch every word that fell from Mam Maggie's lips.

"Dey is made out o' yo blood. Das de thing I'm talkin bout." She looked back into the fire and appeared to be falling asleep.

"Tell me what you is talkin bout, Mam Maggie."

"It's de good Gawd," the old woman said. "When a tree start to rottin, de fruit of de tree is blighted. So when a woman can't stand her burden, it has to fall on her chile, de chile of her bone and blood. When you ward off de spell from yo own self, it has to fall on de chile of yo blood. De good Gawd is gwine to find a way to git His burden borne. Hit will fall on de shoulders what kin bear it."

Corsetta stood up. Tears began to roll from her cheeks. She knelt and buried her face in Mam Maggie's lap, and her body shook. "Pray Gawd, Mam Maggie, don't let em do dat. Please don't let em. I kin bear all de pain de Lawd want to send me.

But don't let em conjure my chile. He ain't done nothin. I is strong. I don't mind de pain. Please Gawd, send me de burden."

Mam Maggie patted her hair. "Tain't no use to take on so. I ain't thu yit."

Corsetta straightened herself, and with a full, pleading voice spoke: "What kin I do?"

"I is ole an you is young an de good Gawd knows all."

"But what kin I do, Mam Maggie? What kin I do?"

Mam Maggie raised her head. "Stand up and come wid me!"

"Where is we gwine?"

"We's gwine into de woods."

"Is gwine into de woods gonna take de pain offen my chile? If you tell me dat, I follow you wharever you lead me."

Together the two women went out from the house. Mam Maggie led the way. The moon was higher, and bright paths of light extended far into the forest.

"Dis way, chile," the old woman said.

She took a path to the right and the two were soon lost in darkness. For more than an hour they walked without speaking. Only frogs in near-by swamps and June bugs in the tree tops broke the night stillness.

Finally Mam Maggie reached another cleared space in the forest. It was hardly larger than a room, and the light of the moon rested upon its floor. In the center of the space stood an old mulberry tree. Its trunk was gnarled and its branches hung low.

"Dis is de tree, chile," Mam Maggie said simply.

She approached the shadow of the tree and knelt.

"Come wid me, chile, and git on yo knees!"

Corsetta went to her and knelt.

"From dis minute, Corsetta, dis tree b'longs to you. I been savin dis tree for myself, to take de burden off my ole shoulders. But I don't need it no more. What burden de Lawd send me now I kin manage wid mysef. I gib dis tree to you, caze you is young and got a long time to live."

Corsetta wept.

"Raise up yo haid, chile, and look unto de heaben, caze I gwine pray."

Both women closed their eyes and raised their faces to the stars.

"Sweet Jedus and good Lawd, hear me pray. I is ole and she is young. Look down on her face, Gawd, and pass yo blessin upon it. Dis here is her tree and hit kin take her burden. Lift de burden, Gawd, from her and her chile, and blight de tree. Turn yaller de leaves and de flowers of de tree. Take hit offen de flesh, Lawd, and put hit on de flower. Pray Gawd, hear dis prayer, for we is weak and sore afraid, and have mercy upon us pore sinners, for sweet Jedus' sake, Amen."

✿ One of the Darkies

On that chilly morning in the fall of the year when
one of the Darkies rushed into the house and announced to
Mister Preston that Matthew was dying, Miss Adelaide was in
the room and, of course, heard. Matthew? she repeated to
herself as soon as her brother had hurried out. Matthew? Which
one of the Darkies was he? To save her life she couldn't remember Matthew's face. What a queer feeling this gave her! One of
those countless Darkies who lived around the plantation was
at this moment dying, and she didn't know which it was. Most
of the faces she recognized even when she saw them away
from the plantation; and at one time or another she had probably
heard all the names; but she had not the slightest idea which
names belonged to which people. "Matthew, Matthew," she
kept on saying, as if to summon his face before her. And, as a
matter of fact, many faces did appear, those that she saw every
day somewhere about her. But as each hovered there, as though
in a cloud before her eyes, each remained obstinately nameless.
She was obliged to admit that to her they were all "Darkies."
She'd taken them as a matter of course, as if they'd always

Southwest Review 27 (Winter 1942): 207-15.

been here and always would be. Even as she'd been aware of
the boxwood at the front of the house and the fruit trees at the
back, she'd been aware of them belonging here. But now from
this dark, voiceless group one had just stepped forth to attract
her attention.

And it was most disturbing to her that she could not remember his face. She could not tell upon which of the many the
hand of death had now been placed.

She got up and went over to the back window, from which
she could see a great part of the yard and some of the fields
where the Negroes worked. Nobody was in sight. And this
was strange, for Negroes had been picking cotton all morning
in these lower fields. Although the day was chilly, she raised
the window about half a foot and stooped as if to communicate
with somebody outside. But she heard not a sound. Then a few
oak leaves, brown and crisp, made a light scraping sound as
the wind hurried them over the hard-packed earth. Miss
Adelaide looked toward the wood-pile. She remembered that
just a short while ago a man had come to split kindling. Now he
was gone. His ax lay against the chopping block, its blade
shining in the sun. From the wood-pile she looked toward the
meathouse, the barn. Still not a soul.

A sudden feeling of loneliness came over her. She couldn't
remember having felt so much alone in all her life. Everybody
had left her to go see this Matthew die. Everybody. All the
Darkies, and even Preston; something had drawn them from
the fields, the barns, the firesides, had drawn all but her. She
alone remained. That which drew the others seemed not to
touch her. She was outside.

What was she doing on this plantation, anyway? How had
it come about that she was living here among these strange
people—among these Darkies whose names she did not even
know? For a second these questions made her feel dizzy, as if

fact and fancy had suddenly become indistinguishable. Preston? He was real, of course. He was her brother. But what did she know of him? Not much more than she knew of the others, the strange ones outside.

Frightened, Miss Adelaide drew back from the window, wishing somebody would appear. Had the cook left the kitchen? she wondered.

Keeping very still in her chair in front of the fire, she tried to make her thoughts lie quietly. How she wanted to get back the state of mind she'd been in before the Darky came! But it wouldn't come back. The uncomfortable feeling lay somewhere deep within her that she had an issue to meet before she could rest again. She had a matter to explain to herself, and there was to be no quiet until she did so.

Was it right that a person should know so little of others? For a whole year now she'd been living here. She'd come to take the place of her brother's wife. What a sorry job of it she must have made! Yet it hadn't been expected of her that she could fill such a place. One who had traveled the world, lived in hotels who'd had none to seek, none to leave—how could such a one take the place of her brother's wife? What preparation had she for life among Negroes? And yet, Miss Adelaide would always remember the pleasure that her brother's letter had given her— the letter asking her to come here to keep him company if she'd become tired of hotels and traveling and if she wasn't afraid she'd get homesick at night when she had only crickets and frogs to listen to. He'd added that she'd be a comfort to him. And it was this that had touched her as few things ever had. Perhaps because it was the last thing she'd expected him to say. It had given her a strange sensation. She'd thought the time long past when anybody could want her.

Well, in the year that had gone by since then, had she been a comfort? She couldn't tell. She had no way of knowing. But if she hadn't been, it was because she hadn't known how. On the other hand, just to herself, she could say that the year had been something of a disappointment to her. Preston hadn't been the man she'd expected to find, not the brother she'd known. He'd given her the feeling that he hadn't called her to watch him live but to watch him die. She'd soon found that his living had already been done, with somebody else. But she did believe that, if Preston had ever reminded her it was another's place she held, he'd done so unintentionally. "Tempe," Miss Adelaide murmured. Another stranger. This furniture about her had been collected by Tempe. All this had been hers.

Yes, and for forty years her brother had slept with this strange woman. What could she possibly know of this closed world they'd made between them? Putting Preston in bed with Tempe made him seem all the more strange to her, impressed upon her with a chilling sensation how little she herself was able to touch him. Truly, his life had been spent. This was only a period of waiting—until his time came to follow. Wasn't it a little selfish of him to ask her to watch? But thoughts like these got Miss Adelaide nowhere, and she tried not to think them. After all, perhaps she was as well off here as anywhere. She wasn't even sure where she'd go if she left. Back to her travels? What did she call home? Ships? Yes, ships . . . as much as any place. She could truthfully say that the ocean she dearly loved; it had been for her a great source of happiness. A little tingle of warmth and excitement came to her when she thought of returning, of leaving this cold, hostile place—this great shell of a house wherein two other people had already lived out their lives.

She drew her chair a little closer to the fire. No wonder she hadn't known the poor dying Darky; no wonder he was just one of many. If her brother had become a stranger, it was hardly probable that she'd know one of the others. For the

Negroes weren't even supposed to enter her world. They were the background folk, the unknown who worked below, who behind the scenes kept things going.

And what a lot of servants she'd had in her lifetime! Bellboys, clerks, maids, nurses, stewards, waiters—all to be had for a price, all where one needed them. No, she didn't know much about them, either. And many a one had served her in his time, too! But she'd paid them all well. Yet there'd been something about paying them that had kept her from getting close to them. There'd never seemed to be a need for warmth. Actually the times had been few when money hadn't been enough. Indeed, hadn't she often stood in mortal fear of the day she'd lose that money?

Suddenly, then, she was seized by an alarming thought. This unknown Matthew who now lay dying was not only Matthew but the countless others as well, the dead and forgotten, who had walked with and served her in the past. Secure with her money, she'd let life slip by without trying to grasp, without even knowing the need for grasping. And now at her feet another lay dying—one who would remain unknown to her forever.

Miss Adelaide stopped rocking. She was almost overcome by a feeling of futility. She felt helpless and old. How many times hadn't she told herself before that people were happier when they stopped trying!

Surrendering as she had not in a long time to a nameless but almost restful despair, she sat for a great while, not bothering to move except to dab at her eyes and to twist absently the tiny bit of handkerchief she held. Was it too late for her to join the others? she wondered. Would they mind if she came to see Matthew dying? Was it too late for her to know something of this stranger who was passing?

These questions aroused in her a surprising little quiver of hope. She could find out, surely. Amazed by her own sudden boldness, Miss Adelaide took her shawl and went into the yard. She felt as if she were about to make an exciting experiment. Where did Matthew live? She didn't know. But she could tell . . . it would be where the crowd had gathered. She couldn't possibly miss them, for there would be a great number. They who were not strangers to one another, they who belonged here on this plantation, would be together.

The fresh cold air almost took her breath. It was much colder outside than she'd thought. Earlier, as she'd watched the Negroes from her window, she hadn't dreamed it was this cold. The Negroes certainly hadn't shown it; they'd looked comfortable to her. It startled one sometimes to think what they had to put up with. She tightened her shawl about her neck.

Had Matthew been a cotton-picker? she wondered. She looked around at the far-reaching fields, where shortly before men and women had been working. Not a living soul was in sight. Piles of cotton had been left on the sheets at the edges of the fields. Work had been stopped suddenly.

This feeling of being left she didn't like; though different, she believed it worse in the open than in the house. Was Matthew such a beloved one among them that nothing could go on? Even the cook had left the kitchen.

As she approached the gate a bird dog, seeing that she was going through, ran up behind her, was at her heels before she knew it. Her heart jumped and a flush of warmth rose to her cheeks. But when her fright passed she felt ashamed. Certainly there was no need for this! As though to reassure herself that she and the dog understood each other, she leaned over and tried to pat him. But the dog was impatient. He ran forward and leaped up at the gate, showing clearly he had no time for play. Unmistakably rebuked, Miss Adelaide began to pull upon the heavy gate. Into the narrowest crack that would admit his body the dog forced himself; then, free, he bounded off across the field as if he'd long been separated from his pack and had just found the trail. Miss Adelaide, with that empty feeling people have when suddenly abandoned, for a moment did not move. She felt more strangely alone than ever. Even the dog was leaving her outside, answering to something the other strangers round her had answered to. Was it possible that he could be looking for Matthew? Perhaps, even, he was Matthew's dog.

A little farther down the sandy road which now lay sunken and narrow between the heavy, full growth upon the fields, she stopped to rest for a moment and to look about. The exercise had caused her breath to come fast, but the cool October air against her face gave her skin a pleasant tingle. Absently as she stood there she began to pull a stringy fluff of cotton which had burst from its hard brown boll. Then, without thinking, she pulled another and another, reaching each time for a lower boll upon the stalk. In a moment both her hands were full and she couldn't tell that the stalk had been touched. With a little lift of excitement she decided that she could finish one stalk at least. Of all the thousands and thousands around her! She bent over now and started to work in earnest. Surely she could clean one stalk! But the strain of bending over was too great, and the bolls grew too low. For this kind of work she needed a chair. Smiling feebly at the pitiful little pile she'd picked, she shook her head. And *they* picked all day long! What a great part of his life Matthew must have spent here! How did the Darkies stand this back-breaking work? As she looked about at the veritable sea of cotton around her, she was almost overwhelmed. It all had to be picked, boll by boll. And Darkies had been doing it for more than a hundred years. Yes, and in his own lifetime, for bread and meat, Matthew had done his share. He'd started as a child and he'd stopped—this morning. He and the nameless others, the dead no less nameless than the living. What a shocking thought! One boll at a time, over acres and acres. This was more than Miss Adelaide could take in. Ten hours a day. Six days a week. Plowing, planting, picking. Here, before she was born, the long dead and the unknown had worked, under this same sun, within sight of these trees. Now another who had labored here was leaving to join the old and forgotten ones.

Beyond the cotton field, Miss Adelaide stopped at the fence which enclosed the stable lot. The mules were all inside, standing about as if it were Sunday. Some were drinking from a long trough; others were feeding. Miss Adelaide looked at the two or three nearest her. They seemed singularly indifferent to the presence of one so strange, for they slowly turned away from her to drink and feed with the others. One of these mules Matthew had plowed. Did mules know people? she wondered. Would one of these strange beasts ever notice that Matthew had gone? A sudden curiosity seized her. She wished she had somebody to ask: she wanted to know which of these mules Matthew had plowed. She felt that if she could determine this she'd have something definite about him to remember. With her forehead wrinkled and her eyes narrowed against the sun, she looked intently from one mule to another. It was no use. They were all alike. Then, suddenly, there before her eyes, one mule stepped forth from the others. Miss Adelaide could hardly believe what she was seeing. Matthew's mule had come forward. She knew it was Matthew's. She was aware of a quickening of her heartbeat. Powers she knew nothing of had allowed her to see him.

This was the farthest Miss Adelaide had ever walked from the house. If she didn't hurry back now her lunch would be ready, and nobody would know where to find her. It didn't matter if others were late, but she knew that her absence would cause alarm. How like a child she'd been treated.

Then, she remembered. Her lunch wasn't ready. Nobody was at home. The cook had left more than an hour ago. What a strange, unnatural day! She wasn't even to have her meals on time. Such a queer day as this she couldn't recall having seen before. Everybody had run off and left her to wander about this great plantation; no lunch was being prepared for her; and here she was looking at mules in the stable lot. Yes, she and the animals had the plantation to themselves.

Which way had she better look now to find the others? She hadn't the slightest idea. But since she'd come so far, a little farther wouldn't matter. She certainly had no reason to go home.

Slowly she started round the lot, taking the narrow footpath which ran by the fence. At the corner of the lot she turned and came to an abrupt stop. For, across the field, stood the cabin in which Matthew lay dying.

The yard was packed with the Darkies; they'd even crowded the porch and were looking in the windows and the door. Somewhere inside, close to the bed perhaps, was her brother Preston, the doctor for all.

Coming upon the house so unexpectedly, Miss Adelaide had been given a little shock; inside her she could feel her heart beating very fast. Here were the people who had left her. She hadn't been frightened, but she was glad that the last hour was over. Looking back upon it, she didn't mind admitting now that it hadn't been pleasant. With a brisker step and a lighter heart, she hurried on.

But the Darkies round the cabin remained motionless. They had their backs turned to her. At any second now some word was coming from within. For a moment, as she watched this crowd of silent people, it seemed to her that she was looking at a great mural, but a truly wonderful one upon which the figures are about to move and from which voices are about to rise. In the background of the painting, as far as she could see, stretched the dark green of the pine forest; closer, to the right and left, lay the proud fields, swollen with a snowy whiteness; and in the center, under the towering oaks which shaded the yard and kept it grassless, stood the cabin. Everywhere around it the motionless figures were waiting.

So intent, so eager were they to hear from within that they did not see her coming. There was not a sign that they knew she was near.

Truly, she told herself, they did not need her now. This was not the time to go among them. Miss Adelaide stopped. But she'd wanted so badly to—what?

At that second, just as she put the question to herself, she heard a muffled cry rise from the crowd. Like a single bird suddenly released, it hung above the yard and was gone. The figures which had been painted now came to life. A wave of movement passed through them. They pressed closer to the door from which word had come.

Matthew was dead.

Miss Adelaide felt a sudden tightness in her throat. Then she was aware of a feeling of emptiness. There was no need to go farther. She was too late. It was as if the goal toward which she'd set her feet had suddenly disappeared from the horizon, leaving nothing but unbelievable space ahead.

Yes, he was dead. There was no need for her to go on. This Matthew she could never know. She had seen his mule, his cotton field, his dog. But she was not to see him. She was too late. He could never be more than one of the Darkies. He was to remain unknown to her forever.

Slowly Miss Adelaide turned. Now surely it was time to go home.

⚜ Old Man's Gold

Flip was thirteen when it happened. Late one afternoon in the spring Mr. William drove down to the cabin at the edge of the farm and said: "Janey Dee, all your children working in the field?"

"Every last one of 'em, Mr. William."

"Well, I got to take one of 'em home with me."

Flip had been drawing water from the well, but he stopped working, just as everybody else round the cabin did, to hear what Mr. William wanted.

Mr. William saw him standing there holding the dripping bucket and listening and he said, "Come here, boy." And then he said, "Janey Dee, what's that boy's name?"

"Him? Da's Flip."

"He got any sense?"

"Yassuh, I reckon he got—"

Then Mr. William looked at him hard, trying to figure out if he would suit. "Boy, I reckon you'll do about as good as any. Wash yourself good and put you on some clean clothes, then come on up to the house."

"Yassuh," Flip said.

Southwest Review 31 (Autumn 1946): 376-80.

Then Mr. Willaim said: "Janey Dee, I'm going to keep this boy up at the house for a while. Papa's had a bad stroke, and we got to have somebody in the room at night."

"Law, Mr. William," she exclaimed, "if da's what you want wid him, he ain't gonna do you no good a-tall."

"How come?"

"He jes ez skeered er sick folks ez he is a hant."

"Pshaw!" was all Mr. William said, and he drove off.

Silence fell upon the little group. They didn't want to look at Flip, but Flip could feel their eyes on him.

Then Janey Dee said rather harshly: "June Thomas, tote that bucket for Flip. You big enough to start totin'."

His brothers and sisters didn't know what to say to him; neither did his Mama. Flip just stood there.

One little girl, wide-eyed, pulled her Mama's skirt, "Muh, he de ole man wid de beard?"

"Hish yo' mouf, Lizzie."

Flip remembered the old man. He'd seen him three or four times from a distance sitting on the porch in the sunshine. Now Mr. William wanted *him*! All of a sudden the world had turned upside down.

But a little while later, washed and shining, his family watching him down the road, he presented himself at the back door. For a long time he was obliged to wait; not a soul paid him any attention. Nobody noticed his Sunday clothes.

Long after sundown he was still sitting, and Mr. William came out, almost stumbling over him huddled upon the steps.

"Lawd, boy! Why didn't you make a fuss? Well, get something to eat now and come on in. I'll show you what you got to do."

In the kitchen the cook had to prod him: "Eat, boy! Don't poke at dem vittles. Dey better 'n you git at home. An' wipe yo' feet good 'fore you go in."

Then he went inside and stood helplessly, a tiny dark figure in the great hall, until Miss Grace noticed him and carried him to the room, saying: "Is this the boy you got, William?"

The Judge was lying on a big bed, a sheet pulled up to his chin. The room was almost dark. There was a small covered light on a table in the corner. And the mantel had been cleared off to hold the bottles of medicine the doctor had left.

"Now, son, all we want you to do is sleep right here," Miss Grace was saying, and she pointed to a pallet that had already been made at the foot of the bed. "If Papa wants anything he'll call you. The doctor says he'll sleep. But if he wants some water, here's the pitcher and glass. You must run to call me or Mr. William if—why, son, you're too big for that! You're not afraid."

Tears had come to Flip's eyes. He couldn't remember a word Miss Grace had said.

Miss Grace told him there wasn't a thing in the world to be afraid of and that if he wanted her all he had to do was come across the hall.

And so a little while later she left him. And without taking his clothes off Flip got down upon his pallet as quickly as he could and pulled the blanket up over his head.

The old man on the bed was an unknown terror in the shadows of the room. Flip lay breathlessly waiting for *It* to show itself. The thought of his brothers and sisters—lying warm and three in a bed—came to him. Every now and then he had to peep out from under his blanket to make sure that he was really here.

But the old man on the bed was quiet. Flip raised his head just a little. He could hear a steady breathing. It was something he knew, and he began saying to himself: "He's sleep, he's sleep." This made him feel a little better. The old man was asleep now and nothing had happened. Flip breathed easier.

Maybe he would *stay* asleep all night long. Then he began saying to himself, ''Be quiet, ole man; be quiet, ole man.''

So, with the old man breathing softly, Flip finally dropped off. And he lay in a little world of his dreams, far from sick old men, until Miss Grace called him in the morning.

''Did he want anything?''

''No'm.''

''Did he call you?''

''No'm.''

Then, in the light of morning, it occurred to him suddenly to look at the old man at whose feet he'd been sleeping. He took a quick, curious glance, then ran outside. There, realizing all at once what he had done, he struck off for home like a colt, kicking his heels in the sunshine.

The children gathered round him. Even Janey Dee and his Papa came to the cabin door.

''Did you sleep in de room?''

''Sho' I did.''

''Won't you skeered?''

''Naw!''

The children looked at him with admiration.

''You gonna move up to de big house all de time?''

''I speck I is,'' he said and went in the kitchen to breakfast.

All the children noticed that their Mama piled his plate high.

But for a good while the Judge was so weak that he slept most of the time. The doctor came regularly and kept him supplied with medicine. During the day Miss Grace and Mr. William took care of him. And, as Flip lay there on his pallet night after night listening to the old man breathe and nothing happened, he got so he didn't mind it. He even reached the point that he would tip up to the side of the bed and look at the old man and wonder if he knew he was there. Staying there turned out to be nothing at all. The old man didn't even call him for a drink of water.

And during this time Mr. William and Miss Grace began to rely upon him. After they had watched their Father during the day, it was a relief to be able to lie down at night, knowing somebody was with him. They gave Flip a little money and found him some clothes that had been stored in the closet. Miss Grace told him she wanted him to stay nice and clean. He had to stay cleaner than the other children because he was taking care of the Judge.

One morning when he was on his way home, after he'd been staying there for a while, some of the children from a nearby cabin ran out to meet him.

"Dem clothes store-bought?"

"Dey come from a store."

"How much money you got?"

"Ain't counted."

"We knows! We knows!" a little fellow exclaimed.

Flip looked at him in amazement. "How come you know what I got?"

Then they all giggled.

"Whilst you gone, yo' bruvvers counts de money you puts in de jar. Den dey puts it back. Dey say you got fo' dollars."

When he got home Flip looked at the jar, then at his brothers and sisters. The jar was exactly where he'd left it, and his brothers and sisters were busy playing store, using rocks for money. One of these days he was going to give them a nickel apiece.

It wasn't so long after this before things began to change at night. The old Judge started talking a little. Flip had noticed that he'd begun to move about some, but it had never crossed his mind that he could say something to the old man. One night, just before he dropped off to sleep, the old man's voice gave him a start.

"Boy, boy, are you there?"

"Yassuh, yassuh, here I is." He threw off his blanket.

"That's all I want to know."

Even while the words hung in the dark over his head it seemed that the old man had left them and dropped back wherever he came from. Flip had a queer feeling. The old man *knew* he was there, knew he'd been there these long nights when it had seemed he didn't know a thing in the world. That old man, whose toes and folded hands had been holding the sheet up, was now somebody. Things wouldn't ever be just the same.

And not many night passed before there was talking again.

"Bring me some water, son."

Flip jumped from his bed and held a glass out to trembling hands. When the old Judge handed it back, he said, "They call you Flip?"

"Yassuh." How did he know his name?

The old man smiled.

"You stay with me, Flip, and I won't forget you. Take care of me good, son; I won't forget you."

"Yassuh, I ain't goin' nowhere."

Flip looked at the old man. Everybody in the house and everybody in the dark little cabins round the farm had gone to sleep, everybody but them. There wasn't a light anywhere except the soft glow from the table lamp. He didn't know what to say and he felt very strange. Miss Grace was asleep; so was Mr. William. Down in the cabin his Mama and Papa were asleep and all his brothers and sisters. He was the only one up, the only one for the old man to talk to. Then the thought came to him: What would the old man do if he did walk off and leave him?

"I ain't goin' nowhere," he said.

And, then, as if it was his business now, he straightened the blanket out on the Judge's bed and ever so lightly touched the pillow with his dark hand.

That night made a change. Even during the day, when Flip was far away from the house, he thought about the old man in the bed. The old man had said something that nobody had heard but him. People saw him in the day—did he talk then, too?—but nobody knew about him at night. Nobody but him. Sometimes he wondered if he ought to tell Miss Grace. Would she care?

Then one night, sometime later, the old man was restless. But Flip had already gone to sleep.

"You sleep, boy?"

Flip was startled. "Nawsuh, I ain't sleep."

"Come and stand here, where I can see you."

Flip went to the old man's side.

"There's nobody here but you and me. An old man and just a little darky." The old Judge smiled. "They put a little darky here to keep me company. Life carried me a long way; people dropped aside; and a little bit of humanity like you has come up at the last to watch over me. Just two of us are left."

Flip stood silently. Was he going to die?

But the old man smiled. "Get me that box, son, on the table. I haven't forgotten what I said."

Flip brought the box to him.

He put his long thin hand inside and drew out a watch. After looking at it for a moment as if it brought something in particular to his mind, he gave it to Flip. "Don't let anybody take it away, son. Not anybody! I'm going to tell Miss Grace it's yours."

"Lemme see it! Lemme see it!" "Is it yourn sho-nuf?" "Lemme see it now, Flip! Lemme hole it!"

He was the center of an excited little group. He was obliged to hold the watch aloft, for his brothers and sisters were jumping up and down all around him, reaching for it. The littlest of them was singing, "I got some gold in my pocket! I got some gold in my pocket! Can't nobody see my gold!" As she sang she whirled gaily around.

Janey Dee heard the noise, looked at the little group curiously, and, drying her hands on her apron, walked over.

"What in de worl' you got?"

Flip held it up high. It was a wonderful sight shining in the sun.

"Lemme hole dat watch."

Proudfully he handed it over. "He give it to me, Ma! De ole Jedge give it to *me*!" He spoke as if he were still trying to believe it.

Janey Dee looked down at him sharply. "He *give* you this, Flip?"

"Yassum."

She kept looking at him.

Then all of a sudden a strange thing happened. She looked down at the little group. "You chullen, hish!" Then she turned away and began to shout: "Joe, Joe, where is you at? Come here and tend to yo' boy!"

Flip was dumbfounded. The children looked up in amazement; the smallest stopped singing her song.

Joe, pulling up his suspenders, stepped forth from the front door of the cabin.

Seeing his Pa, Flip made a sudden desperate grab for the watch. "He did give it to me! He did too! He give it to *me*!" he shouted. Tears flooded his eyes, and he saw them all around him in a crazy world of mist.

"I ain't going to have them finding Jedge's gold watch in my house. They ain't gonna accuse none of mine."

Joe was holding the watch now, looking at it and then at Flip. "Jedge give you this?" he asked quietly.

"Yassuh," Flip sobbed.

"Miss Grace know it?"

"He say he gwine tell her."

"Did he?"

"I don't know iffen he did. He say he was gwine to."

"You come wid me, Flip. If she know it, you kin keep the watch. You an' me goin' to ask her now."

"I don't know iffen he tole her. But hit's my watch, 'cause he given it to me."

"Le's go, Flip," his father said.

As they started off tears were pouring from Flip's eyes. And his brothers and sisters watching after him down the road did not even say a word to one another.

The cook knew something was wrong. She was standing on the edge of the porch, looking down at Joe and Flip. "How come you bound to see her right this minute?"

"That's 'tween me and her. You tell her I wants to see her," Joe said.

"Well, you mought ez well set down. She ain't got no time to listen to you. I been waitin' here myself for her to tell me what to cook. De Jedge has got wuss off all of suddent, an' she ain't gonna leave him. I got a fire goin' in de kitchen stove wid nothin' to put on it. He ain't gonna last through de night. But do things go on like this, I'm gonna cook what I see." She lowered herself heavily into a chair; then she said reflectively, "He be better off."

Flip and his Papa were looking at each other.

All of a sudden, though cook sat between him and the door, like an outside guard, she didn't matter at all. Flip darted up the steps past her.

"Unh-h!" she exclaimed. "Just 'cause he sleeps—I ain't even—"

Inside, Flip saw that the front door was wide open.

He looked toward the Judge's room. Mr. William was there, too! Standing there in muddy boots.

Had it happened already? His heart was pounding.

Miss Grace and Mr. William glanced at him as if he hadn't been anywhere.

"Didn't he say nothin', Miss Grace? Nothin'?" He was burning so to ask her that it almost surprised him that she couldn't read his mind.

But her face didn't answer.

Quickly, then, he ran back.

His Papa was standing there on tiptoes, paying no attention to cook's rambling, looking this way and that, trying to see round her.

"Give it to me, Pa! Quick!"

For a moment Joe hesitated, looked at cook menacingly, then under his big fist handed up the hidden gold.

Flip ran back into the room. There was no time to lose.

Miss Grace and Mr. William hadn't moved.

With his eyes on them, he slipped the watch on the old man's table.

In a minute she'd see it! He would know! He would know! His heart was bumping with the tick of the mantel clock, now pushed back on a crowded little table.

Down the road a dog barked suddenly. It sounded strange. What was out *there*?

Miss Grace turned.

She was biting her lower lip, not knowing what to do. Then in a gentle voice, as if it made no difference at all, she said, "There's his watch, William. You were wondering where it was." Tears came to her eyes, and she left the room.

A lump rose in Flip's throat, and he went outside. His Papa was standing alone now in the near-darkness at the foot of the steps, like a tramp waiting in the light from a kitchen-door.

"Go home, Pa," he said. "He 'bout to die."

Nobody told him to go home, so Flip just stayed. Nobody even knew he was there. Bright new automobiles stood under the great trees round the house, and people walked back and forth across the porch.

Flip waited near the door opening into the hall where the men were, holding their hats in their hands. In a few minutes some ladies went out of the front door, carrying flowers; and then the preacher, who had just been out to see the Judge a day or two ago, whispered something to the men on the porch.

They came inside; and when the people saw them they stopped talking and backed against the wall.

From the front room then they took him.

Miss Grace, holding to Mr. William's arm, followed. After her came some more people—dressed up in Sunday clothes, all of them quiet. There was just the sound of footsteps on the carpet.

Flip could see them all from the front window. They were standing in a circle under the cedar trees across the road.

Would they have minded, he wondered, if he had gone too?

Suddenly, the edge of the circle broke. In twos and threes people turned away. Flip started. He realized that he'd been in this house alone. His footsteps were loud as he ran through the empty hall, out into the quiet afternoon. On he ran, for there was no reason to stay.

But, suddenly, he stopped. He hadn't been home since it happened; and all at once he could see how it was going to be. His brothers and sisters would be playing in the yard. His Mama would be washing clothes. They'd see him coming down the road, and each would say to the others, "Yon come Flip!

Yon he is now!'' Then they'd fall silent, get mighty busy about what they were doing, and make out they hadn't seen him coming.

Oh Lord, Flip said, why couldn't you let him tell?

Then, down the road a little, Flip saw his dog, wandered from home.

''Speck! Speck!''

The sudden, almost joyful, urgency of his voice filled the air.

Speck was wagging his tail in the tall grass; and Flip ran and threw himself upon him as if he'd never let him go.

❧ For Rosa McGee

Late that afternoon Emily was hurrying across town to her mother's. She'd been waiting for John to bring the car and had left him home to watch the children. What her mother wanted with her right at suppertime she couldn't imagine. For once John would have to wait.

Ten months before, when her father died, she'd promised herself she'd go to her mother's every day. Now, with the thousand things she had to do, she was lucky to get there once a week. What did her mother want? she wondered again.

As she sped on she thought of something her older brother Alex said the last time he came to Warren to see how his mother was getting on. "Emily, mother said she knew that you had your hands full, that you were awfully busy." Well, if her mother had said anything to Alex about seeing her so seldom—and Emily wasn't sure she had—she'd said it in an explanatory way, probably as an answer to Alex's prodding. But she was sorry for thinking this, for she knew it wasn't fair to Alex. He'd done everything in the world to get their mother to come live with him. That was the trouble: you couldn't do for her. She'd

Southwest Review 34 (Summer 1949): 295-301.

kept them children. Even now on Thanksgiving and at Christmas it was she who had the dinners. "Daughter, it's so much less trouble for us than for you." This was probably true. But how was Emily to help? The few times her mother had been to her house, it had seemed to Emily that the dining room was too small and that the silver candlesticks and china she and John got for wedding presents were too new and shiny. Yet, it was nothing her mother did, Lord knows. Just her presence, her out-of-placeness in modern little houses with slick floors, and radios, and white electric stoves. She belonged where she was in that sheltered world with Blue Belle to cook for her, somehow a place insulated against time and change.

In a moment she reached the old residential section of town, where the white houses were and the deep lawns and old shade trees. This was where she'd spent her childhood, and it was like returning to another world.

From the long driveway leading to the house Emily saw the lights shining from all the windows and the balcony over the front door. She felt a little quiver of alarm, drew her car to a sudden stop, and hurried across the veranda.

Blue Belle, her mother's old cook and companion, was standing in the wide hallway. She was dressed in shining white apron and cap. The chandelier lights and all the lamps were burning. There were fresh flowers on the tables.

"Blue Belle, what on earth is the matter?"

"Ain't nothin the matter. Don't look like it, do it?"

"Well, what on earth are you all doing?"

Blue Belle was rubbing the console table with an oiled rag. "We's havin a party, Miss Emily."

"Who's having a party?"

"Your mammy. Miss Addie is. Havin a party for Miss Rosa McGee. I can tell you what she wants wid you. She wants you to fix the salads. Your mammy says I'm so heavy-handed they look lak I sot on the lettuce."

"Why didn't somebody tell me Miss Rosa was coming?"

Blue Belle laughed. "Law, chile, you know you ain't got no time for no old lady like Miss Rosa. Your mammy and me was talkin 'bout her the other night, settin here talkin 'bout the olden days. And your mammy says, 'Blue Belle, I bet Rosa wouldn't mind coming down here for a little while. I'll bet she wouldn't mind.' She set there and thought about it for a few minutes, and, bless Pat, if she didn't get up and call up to Washington on the telephone. Look like all of a sudden your mammy sort of hit on something she wanted to do. You know, I reckon I gits mighty wearin. I was right glad when the idea come to her. Sorter relieved me. I said, 'Law, Miss Addie, what do you mean "mind"? Good as the poor thing loves this town? You know she ain't up there in Washington 'cause she likes it. She'd be livin here today if she had any folks left!' That's the Lord's truth, Miss Emily. I can remember myself when her pappy—they called him Ole Colonel McGee—come mighty near ownin half this town. Them kinfolks up there is nice to her, I reckon, but they can't be but so close. Honey, Miss Rosa come in a hurry and brought two suitcases."

"Where is she now?"

"Don't know where she's at, but I'll bet my peace in heaven on one thing: she done ast about more ole Warren folks than you ever knowed lived."Blue Belle hesitated for a moment, then said, as if it were a disconcerting discovery she'd made: "Miss Rosa done got mighty awkward, Miss Emily."

Emily never heard Miss Rosa's name that she didn't think about the time that she came to nurse her and Alex while their mother went to the Exposition in Norfolk. Alex was big enough to realize that she didn't know what to do with children and almost drove the poor lady crazy. Lord, for how many years had Miss Rosa been living from suitcases, eating at other people's tables, and filling in the momentary gap after the death of a family cousin?

"I'll fix the salads in a minute, Blue Belle."

And she went on back to the downstairs bedroom where she heard her mother's voice, and hesitated at the closed door.

"Here, hold this up!"

"Oh, Addie, I'm not going to take that!"

"Of course you're going to take it. You're my size, Rosa. You're the only person I know who can wear it. Now put it with the others."

"Law, Addie, the only thing I've been invited to in Washington is the Episcopal Church. But, I declare, it's bad to have to use the Lord just to find you some nice people."

Emily heard her mother laugh. "Rosa, what else, in heaven's name, would you use Him for?"

Emily pushed open the door quietly. Miss Rosa was looking at the dress which she held at arm's length. "Addie," she said suddenly, "I could wear this when Cousin Annie's little Margaret gets married."

Emily was given an unpleasant little shock. Miss Rosa was thin as a rail; the old dress she wore was ill-fitting; her pince-nez had become too large for the narrowed face that wore them.

Emily looked at her mother bending over the pile of dresses on the bed. She was every day as old as Miss Rosa. But what was it? Did clothes make the difference? She wore a simple black dress; her white hair was well-groomed; her movements as she dealt with the dresses were calm and deliberate. There was no sharpness, no tautness about her.

She looked at Emily and smiled. And Emily knew what had happened. She had taken Miss Rosa in. She was winding up little affairs of her own, now that she knew that her own two children would no longer need her. She had turned to Miss Rosa. Emily felt a little stab of guilt. Her mother had been lonelier than she knew.

Emily burst out, "Why didn't you tell me Miss Rosa had come to see you?"

Miss Rosa gave a startled exclamation. "Law, bless your heart!" And then she kissed her.

And Emily said, "Well, you two certainly keep your business to yourselves. All this going on—"

"Addie," Rosa interrupted, "this child certainly looks like her father."

"I always thought that, Rosa."

"No, Addie, she didn't used to. It's just lately somehow." And she held Emily at arm's length with her hand on her shoulder. "Exactly like him. Except Alex had dark eyes, almost black." As she kept looking at Emily her eyes suddenly brightened. "Addie, did you ever tell this child what Dr. Moore did to save her life?" She asked this eagerly, looking from one to the other, as if she were bearing a small gift.

"Daughter, you were a sick little thing," Rosa said. "I remember just as well as if it were yesterday. Couldn't keep a thing on your stomach. Not a thing. Finally old Dr. Moore came by—Law, will I ever forget him?—came by and said, 'I'm going to give that baby salt-herring and cornpone.' Daughter, we thought the old man had lost his mind. But, let me tell you, he saved your life." Then suddenly she exclaimed: "Addie, I declare, don't you even remember that?"

Emily saw that her mother was looking at Miss Rosa with sudden interest. Was this recollection—this memory of something they'd possibly forgot—a little triumph not to be denied her as she stood there with her eyes shining?

Finally she answered, "Rosa, how you carry those old things round in your head for so long, I don't see. But you wait till Charlie Wood gets here. He's the only person I know who's got a better memory."

Emily's curiosity was aroused. "Mother, what 'Charlie' Wood are you talking about?"

"Emily, you know Judge Wood. You see him every day of your life, down in front of the drug-store," she said with an air of impatience.

"You call *him* 'Charlie'?"

Her mother and Miss Rosa both laughed.

"Daughter, he's plain old Charlie to us," Rosa said. "Addie, who did the poor thing finally have to go to live with?"

Emily knew "Judge" Wood—the old man with cigar ashes on his vest who sat on the bench in front of the drug-store—the old man everybody greeted familiarly, in a way they wouldn't have dared when he was younger.

How strange that anybody had ever known him other than the way she saw him now!

"Mother, he's much older than you," Emily said.

Rosa broke in: "I can tell you. Charlie Wood started school down at that old Blanford Academy just a year or two before I did. And I'm two years older than Addie—wait a minute. Where'd you put that book you've been pasting together?"

What book? Emily wondered.

Miss Rosa was holding her glasses to her nose and looking round the room. "Here." She took the album from the desk, started thumbing through the pages and calling for Emily to look.

The first few pages were filled with old pictures over fresh captions in her mother's hand. The picture Miss Rosa wanted was all but faded; its border had turned yellow. It was a two-story frame building. At the base of the gable which fitted over the front porch was the black lettering BLANFORD ACADEMY. Under this the pupils sat in four rows on the steps, long-haired girls with high-topped shoes and big boys in white stiff collars. "This was the whole school," Miss Rosa said thoughtfully, then added: "I declare, we certainly do look pitiful."

"Miss Rosa, do you remember them?"

"Honey, not all."

For Emily it was a closed world.

"There's your mother," Rosa said, holding her finger under a tiny figure on the bottom row.

"Mother!" Emily exclaimed. "Poor thing, you look like an orphan."

Miss Rosa's finger moved up a row. "There I am—whew-h—Addie, what did our parents make our clothes out of? Gunnysack? Look! There's Charlie Wood right there. Look here, Addie, at Charlie's ears—always had the biggest I ever saw! Addie, isn't this Bessie?"

"Mother, where was this place? Here in Warren? I never heard of it."

"I don't suppose you have, daughter. That place was torn down long, long before your day. It was way out there at the end of Pickett. There's a gin there now and a warehouse."

Emily was disturbed. More had happened during the past months than she knew. This call for Rosa; this concern with old pictures. Then she thought again about what her brother Alex had said. He'd stayed here in the house for a week. This fact seemed suddenly significant. Had he discovered something Emily had missed? She looked at her mother thoughtfully. Was that strong pattern, familiar and as old as her own life, wearing now? That pattern which was to hold forever? Emily felt her heartbeat quickening. Yes, her mother knew. Her mother had been knowing for—oh, how long?

"Miss Emily," Blue Belle put her head in the door. "You better come on here and fix them salads. It's pretty near time for them folks."

Rosa was brought back to the moment. "Law, Addie," she exclaimed, "I think I'll wear that dress! They haven't seen me in years."

Blue Belle stood there for a moment, then turned slowly away. Emily followed along behind her.

Emily was conscious of a vague sort of agitation, as if she'd been set suddenly upon an unfamiliar lonely road. What remained for her to see?

"Blue Belle, who else is it besides Judge Wood?"

"Honey, nobody but ole Mrs. Moseley. She been on your mammy's mind. Tell you the truth, Miss Emily, a good meal will do her good, the way she has to live."

"Was *she* a friend of theirs?"

"Not exactly a friend, I don't reckon. Just sorter belong to the same day. Lately your mammy been talkin to her over the telephone."

"I never heard mother say anything about Mrs. Moseley or Judge Wood either."

"Well, this party will do 'em all good. Though spareribs sure don't look like no party to me."

Emily saw the spareribs ready for serving. And a big pan of blackberry dumpling. "What on earth?"

"Your mammy told Miss Rosa to name the dish, whatever in the world that could be got. 'Law,' Miss Rosa said, 'spareribs!' Said that when she was up there in Washington she used to think about spareribs in Warren. 'Just have one big dish.'" Blue Belle turned to look at Emily as if something had just occurred to her. "Reckon they'll taste as good as she thought they would when she was in Washington? Now you hurry up wid the salad. Them folks is probably here."

As she hurried with the salads and vegetable dishes for Blue Belle to serve, she was conscious of the fact that the little group had come to hold a strange fascination for her, as if she were about to glimpse something long withheld. Somehow, this was so unlike her mother who for so many years had been there to do and do for them.

When Blue Belle came back in a few minutes to say that they all had come, Emily was aware of a strange sort of urgency to allow no more to escape her. Quickly she dabbed dressing on the salads, then tiptoed up to the swinging door that stood between her and the little group in the dining room. The very names she heard had the effect of estranging her. Rosa, Charlie, Addie, Sue. Not her mother, nor Judge Wood—but people they'd once been. "Rosa, you weren't there. . . ." "Charlie, you remember. Tell how it was!"

It was the old man talking now, reaching back to a distant day. Oh, how little they who saw him knew what lay within!

"No, no, Rosa, that wasn't the way! The time we're talking about you weren't even there. Addie, you remember, I took Adeline. Adeline McCall."

"Charlie Wood!" Mrs. Moseley exclaimed. "Adeline McCall?"

Emily's mother laughed at the astonished voice of Mrs. Moseley.

"Never heard in my life that you ever courted her!"

It was as if the discovery now put her out, and they all laughed aloud.

"How in the world I missed that!"

"Lawd, Sue, if Margaret hadn't come along I'd have married that girl."

Rosa said, "Pshaw, Charlie, you wouldn't have done any such thing! I could read your mind better than a book: Addie, did you ever once think that Charlie would marry Adeline?"

"Law, Rosa, Charlie didn't know his own mind."

"Let me finish," Charlie said. "Addie, it was me and Adeline and you and Alex. Alex had just come to Warren—doggone if I didn't introduce you to him. Long-legged, dark-eyed, always just like he'd stepped out of a bandbox."

Breathlessly Emily heard this reference to her father.

". . . I thought Alex could handle a boat, and he thought I could. . . ."

Emily's mother laughed, remembering a picture, Emily realized, that no other could see.

"The wind was with us, I suppose, because we sailed off well enough. Anyway, I certainly didn't know that Alex didn't know any more than I did. . . ."

"I don't see why you didn't!" Emily's mother broke out defensively. "Till he came to Warren, Alex had never been near the water!"

Emily thought about the letter she'd accidentally discovered when she was a girl that her father had written her mother before they were married. She had the same feeling now—that it was a thing she'd no right to see.

"Anyway, we got that thing about three miles off. I looked at Adeline, and, bless me, she was white as a sheet. She could hardly whisper: 'Let's turn back, Charlie.' Tell you the truth, I'd been thinking the same thing, but I was leaving it up to Alex—to do the tacking or whatever you call it. But, bless Pat, he looked at me as if to say, 'Well, go ahead!' By George, the second I looked at him I knew we were sunk. I said, 'You go ahead.'"

"Charlie," Emily's mother said, "if I hadn't been too young to have any sense I never would have got in that boat in the first place. I knew Alex didn't know."

Charlie laughed again. "Yessir, that was some picture we made when they had to come to get us. A fine way to win a girl!"

He chuckled to himself.

"Well, that's news to me," Mrs. Moseley said again, still a little put out. "I never heard before in my life that you courted Adeline. And I thought I knew everything going on."

"Lawd, I knew, Sue," Rosa said.

Was Miss Rosa out of it even then? Emily wondered. Hadn't she ever had a beau of her own?

Emily's mother said, "Charlie, there's one more thing. Sue, you remember this, I know. The night the old school burned—"

"Miss Addie, I remembers that myself," Blue Belle stopped

serving to put in. "Night they thought all the colored folks' houses was going to catch. Had us standing out in the road wid all our truck piled round us, just standing there looking at the sparks flying. Nothing to throw water wid but buckets."

"Oh, oh," Judge Wood exclaimed. "That reminds me! That reminds me!" Then he went on as if it had suddenly returned to him. "Tom Weaver was volunteer fireman. He brought you down. When have I thought of Tom! Tom was trying to cut Alex out! Was up at your house when the fire started. Yessir, you came to the fire with him. Alex knew it, Addie! Alex knew it!" he sang out gleefully.

"Now, Addie," Mrs. Moseley said, "that's something I did hear—about you and Tom. I knew that."

"No such thing," Emily's mother said. "No such thing."

"For heaven's sake, Addie," Miss Rosa said. "Don't sit there and deny it."

Tom Weaver? It was a name she'd never heard.

Emily then drew quietly away. There was no need to say that she was leaving, for they'd forgotten she was there.

Could it be that nothing was ever lost? she wondered. Wasn't there a day of one's past that wasn't somewhere alive?

She went out to her car to begin the drive home, back to her husband and children. How strange that all of this could lie buried for so long, that her mother and Miss Rosa and the others had been carrying it with them, and that it was still so fresh and strong through the years.

Her thoughts went back to her own early youth, to the time in college that she was going to marry Bryan. And a rather startling thought came to her. Even this, that early love—yes, it was love—even this would never be lost. And now she knew that it lay buried in half a dozen minds—Margaret's, Kate's, Frank's, and Bob's. Wherever they were they remembered. They'd been there and they'd known. It was of John they'd never heard. Had John ever heard of Bryan? she wondered. For the life of her she couldn't remember. How strange this seemed.

To every place on earth now had gone those dim little figures of school days, and each of them held some part of her as did she of them. What was the little girl's name who'd copied from her paper and had been sent to the principal? Sally? Sally Clark. Emily could see her now. Oh, where was she?

When she walked into the house she found John waiting.

She looked at him, half expecting him to ask what in the world she was thinking, for she'd never been able consciously to deceive. Could he have heard? she wondered again.

"John," she said.

He looked up from his paper.

"Have you—have you—put the children to bed?"

He looked at her curiously. "No, Emily, it isn't time."

Then she walked quietly by, his eyes following her.

At the end of the hall her children were playing; and she stopped and for a long moment looked thoughtfully down upon them.

❧ The Shade of the Grove

Flip had never said a word to Mr. Ed, for Flip lived on the edge
of the plantation, in the cabin farthest away from the great
central grove, which somewhere beneath in its green shade hid
Mr. Ed's white house, his comings and goings, and the doings
of all the little company, black and white, who surrounded
him. The grove rose up, green and billowing, out of the broad
flat fields, like a great circus tent tossing and swollen with
wind. In summer, the roads leading to it, little rivers of sand,
were lost between the far-stretching fields. But in winter when
the fields were bare, when the cotton stalks stood thinly, bleak
and stripped, uncovering the earth beneath them, the roads
stretched out, threads of a giant web, holding the grove at the
center to the far limits of pine woods. But Mr. Ed's house and
grove were only a distant part of the background of Flip's little
world, part of the barrier between him and the earth beyond.

Flip had never spoken to Mr. Ed, but every day from a distance he saw him drive by. For every day Mr. Ed took a drive
around the plantation. He rode around in the buggy with Josephus holding the reins at his side. Summer and winter this

Southwest Review 36 (Autumn 1951): 291-97.

drive was a fixed core of certainty in the passage of the long days—the one event which gave official stamp to the expiration of the half-day. The time of any happening was established according to its relation to, before or after, Mr. Ed's passing. "Has he gone yit?" "Happened 'bout an hour 'fore he come by." If, as on some rare occasions, he came by an hour or so late when morning had actually passed into noon, morning still seemed there, impatient, a runner awaiting notice to leave. Daily schedules were planned to fit the hour he'd appear. "I'm gonna see kin he spare me 'bout ten more dollars this Sadday." "Want to show him where the roof been leaking." "Wisht I could git Josephus to drive him by my shed. Plum near broke down!"

The inspection trip was a daily tribunal. As binding and as real as in any court of law were the sentences handed down from the buggy and received upon the roadside. Quarrels were settled. Darkies turned away from the buggy unquestioningly, weighted, perhaps relieved, with the knowledge of a final law.

There was hardly a spot on the whole plantation from which you couldn't follow the progress of the tour, even though sometimes there was nothing more to see than a faint cloud of dust hanging above the green fields, hovering there when the buggy had stopped like a shadowing cloud, and trailing sluggishly behind when the buggy was in motion, a fantastic ever-changing balloon pulled by unseen revelers in a rustic Mardi Gras. But then the darkies could see it above the green fields and could figure about when he'd get to them.

Mr. Ed would start on North Lane—longest and straightest of all the plantation roads—which led directly from the front of the house to the county highway. But he'd turn off just short of the public road and begin the long sweep around. Josephus was the only possible driver, for he knew instinctively the gait that was wanted for the best view of the crops in their progressive stages of growth: hardly more than a walk while the cotton was young and the hands in colored dress were chopping grass, a lively trot for the plant in bloom, and sometimes a full stop for Mr. Ed to get out and examine the bolls when first reports reached him of opening squares. Josephus knew, too, what time could be spared the hands, standing in little groups of twos and threes, who were waiting ahead as far as they could see. Complaints, problems, even tragedies had been classified by him as to their claim upon Mr. Ed's time. For Josephus, as well as Mr. Ed, had time and time again heard the full roster of plantation ills, and there was no single one of them to which he couldn't assign its relative gravity. There were times too when Josephus' own impatience, his own disgust, asserted themselves, and he arbitrarily cut the sessions short by reaching for the whip and giving a sharp "cli-cup" from the side of his mouth. But Josephus had for so long identified his own reactions with those of Mr. Ed that it rarely occurred to him that he was exercising independence of judgment.

Josephus knew, however, that Mr. Ed wouldn't tolerate any obvious intervention; he was, therefore, obliged to constrain himself to such oblique methods of protecting him from his tenants that the tenants were more often aware of them than was Mr. Ed himself. Josephus wouldn't tolerate a lie, and he was constantly on guard to expose them. "Speak up, Man, so he kin hear you better," he would say. Whereupon the rebuked and marked man would be obliged shamefully to repeat his falsification, knowing that Mr. Ed had been alerted, for Josephus' command was indeed a signal that Mr. Ed had learned long ago to rely upon, although there was no possibility ever of the recognition of the existence of an unspoken language between them.

And so it came about that the darkies began to discern in Josephus their final subtle judge. And though they unfailingly stood on Mr. Ed's side of the buggy and looked up at him, they were far more careful to address Josephus' sensitive ear.

It would greatly have surprised all the darkies to learn that in the intervals between stops, when there was about the two only the play of the summer wind, seldom did there pass between them a single word.

So it was that little Flip had seen Mr. Ed every day, had stood namelessly, his bare toes in the dust, in a wide-eyed little group of brothers and sisters, somewhere discreetly back of their parents who'd stepped forward to the roadside like chieftains in counsel for the remainder of a small dispirited tribe.

But it came about one afternoon in August that Flip spoke the last words Mr. Ed was to hear upon this earth and that the little boy in turn heard the last words Mr. Ed was to speak.

It was Saturday afternoon, and Flip had been sent to the grove by his Pappy to deliver a chicken to Mr. Willie Boone. Mr. Boone, according to an unfailing shrewdness of judgment on the part of the tenants, had acquired, during his comparatively brief stay on the plantation, a ranking of third place in the hierarchy of plantation rule. The fact that his little dominion of authority was unknown to Mr. Ed did not in any way invalidate its very real, though shadowy, existence. Mr. Boone worked upon a practical level of giving and receiving favors, even though the favors he had to give were his by virtue of his being in the one position to give them without attracting Mr. Ed's attention. The darkies on the plantation did not resent Mr. Boone. The position he held had to be filled. A much less amiable person could have filled it, for many a one had.

So little Flip, innocent agent of intrigue, came up bearing a chicken from his father to Mr. Boone.

When the little boy stepped from the warm afternoon sun

into the ragged shade at the edge of the grove, he stopped for a moment, shifting the chicken from under one arm to another, as though some special manners were required now, similar to the head-baring demanded of the children in the cool damp entrance to Rising Star Chapel. And indeed on this Saturday afternoon the grove was as dark and as quiet as a church. The shaded, clean-swept earth was cool to Flip's feet, and nowhere about could he see a living soul.

Flip had never thought consciously of Mr. Boone before. But now that he held a chicken that had to be got rid of, one, in fact, that had to be put in Mr. Boone's hands, for his father had said, "Don't give it to nobody but him," Flip had to think of him as a person who had to have somewhere a place to eat and sleep. Belonged *somewhere* in the grove, but not at Mr. Ed's. There ought to be somewhere a place in-between.

Flip, then, as though seeing the grove for the first time, looked about with an appraising eye at all the little white-washed cabins—now closed and smokeless—built in a cluster like so many gray setting hens in tall grass under the dominating shadow of the larger house. Smokehouse—chicken-ouse—. Flip was at a loss to know where Mr. Boone belonged. A house was missing in the scale.

Flip stood helplessly in the middle of the yard, a tiny figure with his chicken. The only sound on earth was the rustling of the over-arching branches of the great oaks and elms, from beneath which he couldn't even see the sky.

"Boy!"

Flip jumped, turning to look back the way he'd come, for he hadn't known a soul was following.

"Boy!"

He turned again, looking across the empty yard.

Soft, impersonal, not like his Pappy's or any voice he knew, it seemed to come from the earth itself.

"Up here."

And there across the vacant yard, just above the back porch railing, veiled now with clematis, decorated like the bandstand in town on the Fourth of July, he could see the top of Mr. Ed's white head.

With a motion more mechanical then deliberate, the little boy got the chicken behind him. His own presence here, he felt vaguely, was somehow wrong. But the chicken, he knew instinctively, was additional guilt.

"Step here."

Flip was standing motionless, knowing that he couldn't run. For Mr. Ed's voice was the most strangely compelling sound he'd ever heard. It wasn't like hearing just a man. For Mr. Ed, ever since the child had known anything, had been the unquestioned, unquestionable Law . . . which, Flip vaguely perceived, held together somehow the little world in which he lived. Mr. Ed was as impersonal, as untouchable a thing, hovering upon the horizon of the child's life, as was the rising and setting moon. That he hadn't always been there and that he wouldn't always be, couldn't have dawned upon the child's mind. Flip had no more choice now than he would have had if the Jesus had spoken that Brer Stanley talked about. In fact, Flip reckoned that Mr. Ed was who Jesus looked like.

Burdened with guilt, the little boy stepped forward, the chicken at his back resisting the terrible grip he was giving it. He was terror-stricken for fear it would manage to cackle.

Short of the porch he stopped, a respectful distance between them, awaiting sentence from the old man who was sitting behind the white clematis that seemed to have spilled from the rail.

"Come on," the old man said.

The child turned then to the steps, shifting the chicken with every step, as though it were a needle holding position in a turning compass.

Now that Flip could see all of him, Mr. Ed was sitting in a rocker, his cane lying across his lap. He was resting his head against the back of the chair. And Flip had always thought he was a big man! There were flies, too, around his hands. Maybe this wasn't Mr. Ed.

"What's your name, son?"

"Flip."

"Flip?" he said, as though it were a very little thing he'd find in a minute but had to think where he'd placed it.

"Flip. Tim Weeks' boy," the child said.

But the effort seemed to be lost, for it was as if the one familiar thing that the child had to show the old man wasn't recognized.

But the old man said in a minute, "Is your chicken tied?"

"Suh?"

The little boy's heart gave a jump, and he stretched his fingers to reach for the chicken's neck.

"If it's tied, you can put it down."

"Nawsuh, I mean yassuh," for he didn't know what he meant.

"Just put it down, son, it won't get away."

So the little boy eased it to the floor, his face burning with shame. It was like standing naked in a crowd.

And Flip had to keep reminding himself that it wasn't stolen, for he'd actually got to feeling that it was, his reason for having it in the first place having become blurred in his mind.

But Mr. Ed wasn't even looking, didn't even care whether he had a chicken or not.

And the little boy stood there, his wonder growing at the silence he received.

Was Mr. Ed 'sleep? he wondered.

The flies settled now upon his hand, and Mr. Ed didn't even wave them off. His hands were folded, a little mountain in his lap.

And suddenly the little boy had a strange feeling. This wasn't Mr. Ed! The only Mr. Ed he knew was the big man everybody waited for along the roadside who could think a minute and settle every trouble that came up, who kept folks from fighting and fussing, and who kept practically all the money there was in the world somewhere up at the house. The old man you saw from a distance across the fields riding under the noonday sun with Josephus sitting beside him to help him in and out of the buggy, standing there waiting and helping without so much as putting a finger to his arm.

Flip couldn't explain it but he knew in his heart that this wasn't Mr. Ed. Mr. Ed wasn't something *he* talked to and looked at real close while he was 'sleep like everybody else. Mr. Ed had already passed into a memory—into a bright picture of a man in a buggy under the sun. Flip wasn't going to try to connect this old man with that picture—the old man sleeping now with the flies on his hand. This old man didn't fit at all, and Flip didn't any more know what to do with him than with a stranger he'd stumbled on lying in a ditch.

Must he wake him? Must he give him a drink from the well?

He started to speak, hesitated, then softly: "Mr. Ed," knowing even before the words formed there'd be no answer.

But surely he couldn't leave him, for somebody ought to watch.

The little boy picked up a folded newspaper then, and slowly began to fan the flies away.

It had seemed to Flip a little while ago that everybody on the farm had gone to town, leaving him alone with Mr. Ed. But now the darkies were coming from every direction. There was one big crowd at the back porch steps, and there were smaller groups, mostly women holding to their children to keep them quiet, waiting at the edge of the grove for their men to come back and tell what had happened.

Flip himself was the center of the group of men, having to tell over and over again exactly how it was. Flip's Pappy, straight and proud, was standing back of him, one hand resting on the child's shoulder, a chicken under his arm.

It had seemed so little a thing to Flip while it was happening, and now all of a sudden it was so much! As he repeated it now over and over, trying to answer unexpected questions about things they kept telling him he must have seen, he had a queer feeling that they weren't talking about the same thing. Nothing so important as they made it could have happened to him.

But getting a glimpse of it through the eyes of the grown-folks around him was like seeing his own Mammy shouting that day he climbed up to the meetin' house window.

Flip thought Mr. Ed was 'sleep was all, he had said to them again and again. So he just stood there fanning the flies away till somebody came up. Thought maybe Josephus had stepped off to get him some water. There was the newspaper right there on the edge of the porch, one he fanned him with. (And the crowd turned curiously to peer at it.) Didn't know how long it was, it didn't seem so long, before Mr. Willie Boone come up, a-toting a watermelon, looking lak he mought drap it and bust it 'fore he set it down. Didn't see 'em till he was plum on the porch, then looked up all of a suddent, his eyes about to pop out.

"What in the name er Gawd?"

"And I say, 'Mr. Ed 'sleep.'"

"Then he come running, knowing better, and just standing there over him, looking down."

Somebody broke in to demand of the crowd, "Whar in de worl is Miss Julia at?"

"Man, you know she at Holly Hill, and dey done sont Will

Gee to git her."

"Den what, Flip?"

"Den Mr. Willie Boone say, 'Boy, is he daid?'"

"Den Flip say. . . ." The story was taken up now by the older ones who'd heard it all before. "Den de boy he plum near jump off dat porch. Dat boy didn't think Mr. Ed was nothin' but 'sleep. Flip back off, bumping into dat watermelon Mr. Boone done left plum in de middle of de floor.

"Den Mr. Boone was bendin' down, kotched up his hands to feel his pulse and pressin' his head down close to see what he could hear. He looked up in a minute lak dare was a crowd of folks waiting. And he said real sad-like to nobody but Flip, 'De most I kin say of Mr. Ed is dat his heart ain't stopped.' And tears began to trickle down his cheek like it was a private thing between him and Mr. Ed that wouldn't nobody ever know about."

"Tell me, where in de worl was Josephus, how-come he warn't close by?"

"If anybody had ever ast me, I'd a-said when de time come, Josephus wuz gwine be wid him."

But the main thread of the story was taken up by Seth—the first of all the tenants who happened along.

"I thought I seen something funny this afternoon. The more I thinks about it, the more I wonder. I was jist standing by that little garden patch I got, seeing how all my cabbage was full of BB shot, so et up wid bugs—standing in that patch there ain't much going on in the grove that you can't see—and all of a suddent I seen Mr. Ed, standing down there by hisself near the old kitchen. That warn't like him, walking around two o' clock in the day, hot as it was. Josephus warn't wid him, warn't nobody. Ast Lula didn't I mention I wonder how-come Mr. Ed was out. He walked real slow from de kitchen to de smoke-house. And ever now and then he'd stop, both hands folded on his cane out in front of him, and look across the fields. Took a long walk, too, plum round the grove. Looking at him, thin like he was and leaning on that cane, give me, more I think about it, a real funny feeling. Reckon what did Mr. Ed have on his mind?"

Seth looked about at his crowd of listeners, silent now with this last image of Mr. Ed.

"My Ma got a warnin' befo the good Lawd took her," one spoke, holding before himself some little memory of another time. "And if anybody ever lived was close to Jesus, my Ma was."

"Hit was a little favor the Lawd done him was what it was."

"Well," Seth went on, "seeing him like that got on my mind, so I say to myself 'Seth, how-come don't you stroll up there, see what 'tis?' Lula noticed me setting off. Ast her didn't she think it was something curious. She say, 'Seth, where in de worl is you going to now?' Well, I come on. And hadn't hardly got to the grove fo' I seen Mr. Willie Boone on de porch wringing water out of what looked lak a dish rag. Then I couldn't see Mr. Ed on account of this vine on de rail. And there was this here child—" he looked about to designate Flip, but not seeing him in the crowd immediately, went on—" jist standing there. I don't know how in the worl Mr. Boone seen me so quick, but he did. First thing I know, he was waving his hand at me, hollering, 'Come here, quick, Ephraim.' I knowed he was talking to me, waving at me, but as good as he knew me he was calling me somebody I don't nowhere near bear no favor to. I knowed 'twuz something wrong, cause I knowed he hadn't seen me good. I lit out, then, running. And all I could think about was seeing Mr. Ed walking round that grove by hisself. I knowed good as I know my name that it was something that done happened to him. I warn't surprised none when I got there, 'fore I seen him good, and heard Mr. Boone say, 'Help me lift him easy into the house.'

"He was so little lying back in his rocker I coulda almost not knowed who he was. We took him real gentle, Mr. Boone on one side, me on the other. One of us coulda carried him. Wouldn't you-all a-thought Mr. Ed was a bigger man than that?"

"Reckon who's wid him now?"

"Ain't nobody but Mr. Boone. And if Miss Julia gits here as quick as she can, hit's gwine be nigh onto midnight."

While they were talking, a lone figure came silently from the kitchen to the back steps. It was old Della, the cook. A hush fell over the crowd. For a minute or two, Della stood there, looking out across the yard, not seeing the men. She hadn't turned the lights on in the kitchen. There was no play of firelight on the floor from the wood range. She sat down on the bench against the wall. If she knew the men were there, there was no sign.

The little group at the steps drew respectfully back into the yard. One of them whispered: "She been cookin' his supper for twenty years."